this book
belongs to:
from:

INTRODUCTION

What you are holding in your hands is the very first book from a special little girl. Makayla Joy Sitton began reading at the age of two and absolutely adored books and storytelling.

"The Bear's Castle" came about in a most unique way. We homeschooled Makayla and would often record her voice as she recited literature she had memorized, like Bible verses and poems.

One day, we asked Makayla to just tell us a story. She was only six years old when out of her imagination sprung this sweet tale of a little bear who builds a castle and befriends a unicorn.

Providentially, we captured Makayla's impromptu telling of this story on audio tape just several months before she went to Heaven.

We cherish hearing Makayla using her various inflections and voices which she created especially for her characters. "The Bear's Castle" has now become a precious treasure for our family as we hope it will be for yours.

Children's storybook illustrator, Tyler Hollis, reached out to us after hearing of our Thanksgiving Day tragedy. She too has suffered the death of a daughter and could relate to our heartache. After reading about Makayla's love for books and storytelling, Tyler graciously offered to illustrate and publish Makayla's story about the little bear. We are forever grateful to Tyler for helping to make Makayla's dream come true.

Her Mama had always told Makayla that she might be an author one day. At only six years old, at last she is one. May you and your family be blessed by reading this book together, remembering that it comes from a faith filled little girl who loves the Lord and the beautiful things in life.

As parents, we know how much little ones love to hear other children read and tell stories. So we decided to include the audiobook of Makayla telling her story of "The Bear's Castle". May this sweet, simple story bring you and your children many precious moments together.

God's grace to you all...

Jim and Muriel Sitton

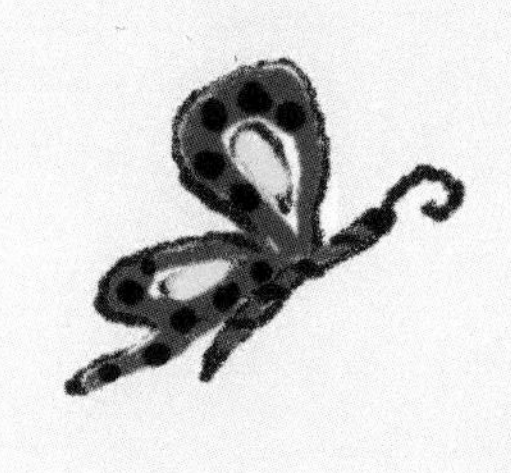

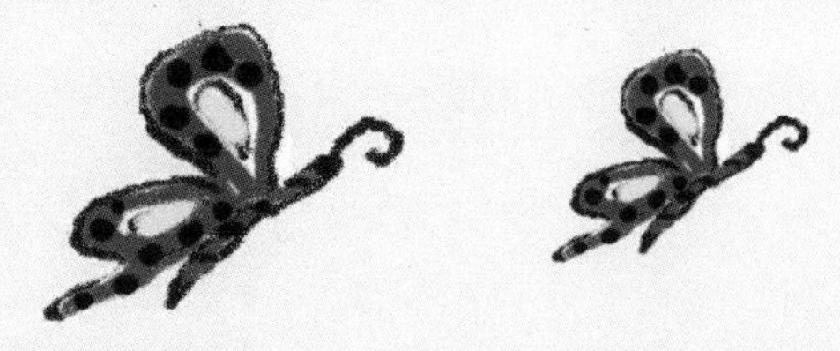

Makayla
Joy
Sitton

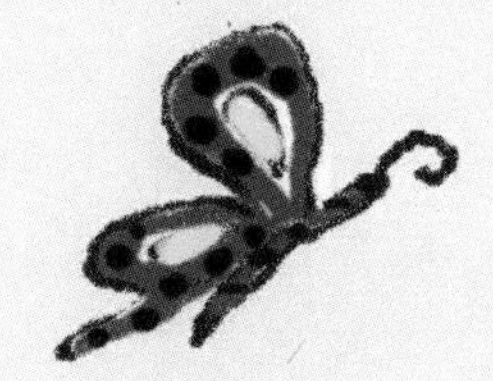

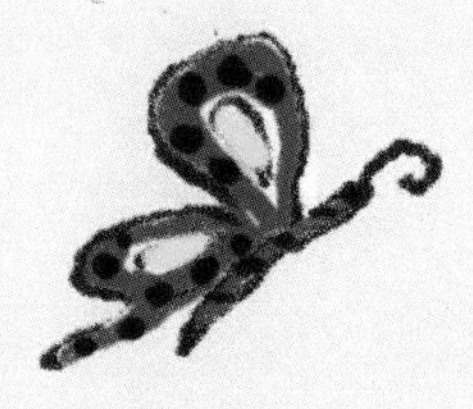

THE BEAR'S CASTLE

ISBN:1452867747 / 9781452867748

This book was printed in the United States of America.

Illustrated and Published by: Tyler Hollis
www.childrensbookillustrator-tylerhollis.com

Author: Makayla Joy Sitton

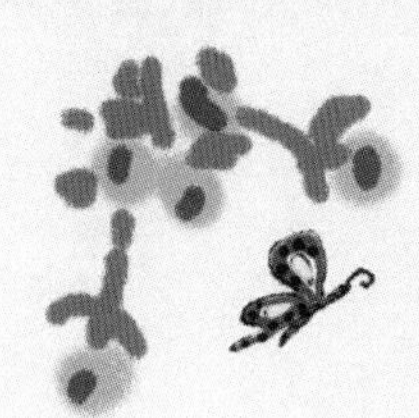

DEDICATION

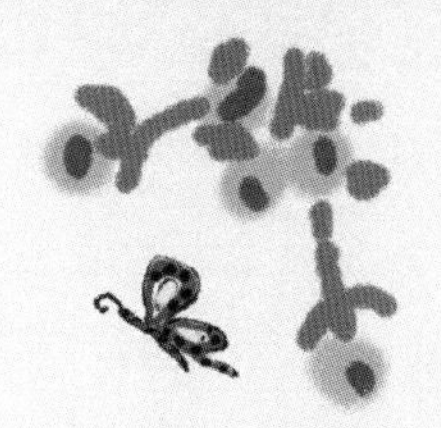

In loving memory of our precious daughter,
Makayla Joy Sitton...

Sweet Pea, we love you and are so very proud of you. You continue to shine your light and love for the Lord in everything you say and do. Thank you for inspiring us all to cast our eyes on beautiful things.

With hearts forever knitted together as one...
Your Mama and Papa

٢

THE BEAR'S CASTLE

by Makayla Joy Sitton

Illustrated by Tyler Hollis

The book and CD may be purchased at www.makaylajoysitton.com

Once there was a little bear who wanted to make all his wishes come true. And so he asked his mother, "Mother, may I please make a Bear Castle?"

HONEY
Honey Weat
FLOUR
JAM
SODA
COOKIES
Tea
KISS the COOK

"A BEAR castle," said his mother. "What are you talking about?"

"A castle where I and my friends can live happily ever after," said the Little Bear.

"Well, uh, go ahead if you'd like," said his mother.

And so Little Bear, as he was called, got lots...

and lots...and lots...

and LOTS of mud!

And he packed it into big little bricks. And he put them in the sun...

just like the Egyptians did. That was the *only* way bears knew how to make bricks anyway.

So, the Little Bear went,
after his nap...

afterward he went to his little corner where ALL the bricks were drying. And do you know what he saw?

He saw the CUTEST little Unicorn sitting right there among the mud!

"Hello," said the sweet little lady Unicorn. "What are you doing with the bricks?"

"I am going to make them into a castle!" Little Bear said.

And looking thoughtfully at the Unicorn he said, "I wonder, do you know that I read in my fairy tale book that some castles have Unicorns in them!?"

TALE OF THE UNICORN
ONCE UPON A TIME
A PRINCESS AND A
UNICORN LIVED
IN A CASTLE

"Why I'm the *perfect* Unicorn!" exclaimed the lady Unicorn.

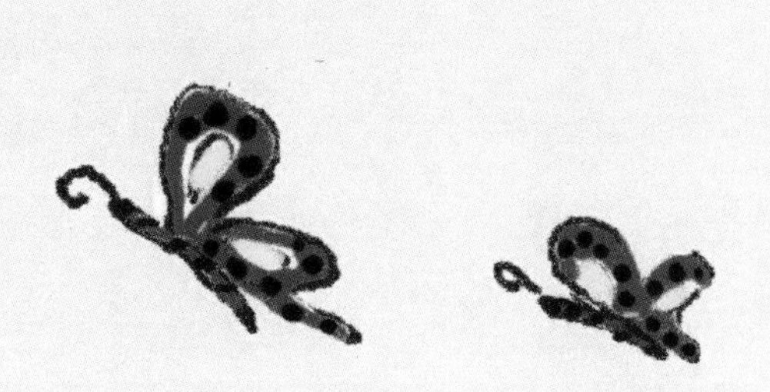

And so Little Bear, and the Unicorn lived happily in their castle -after it's finished of course- ever after.

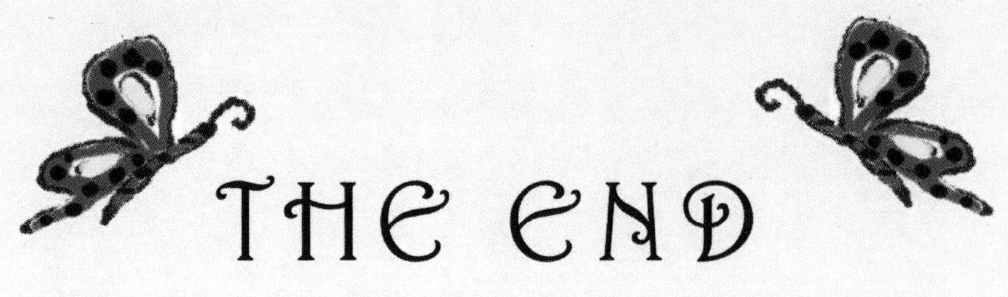

THE END

LITTLE BEAR'S CASTLE
Friends Welcome!

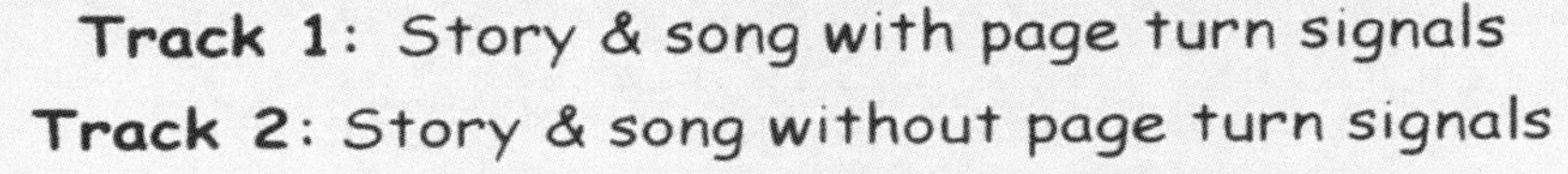

Track 1: Story & song with page turn signals

Track 2: Story & song without page turn signals

FOREVER FRIENDS

Forever friends, happ'ly ever after
Forever friends, caring we'll be
Bears and unicorns, castles and laughter
Forever friends, ever we'll be

Your forever friend, God is always watching
Holding your hand, guiding your way
As you walk along, strong and courageous
Forever friend, with you each day

Unicorn castles, unreachable dreams
Nothing's impossible as it seems
Always keep reaching, keep trusting
Keep hope in your heart, your heart

Forever friends, happ'ly ever after
Forever friends, caring we'll be
Bears and unicorns, castles and laughter
Forever friends, ever we'll be
And precious in God's eyes, always you'll be

Words and Music by Sandra Baran

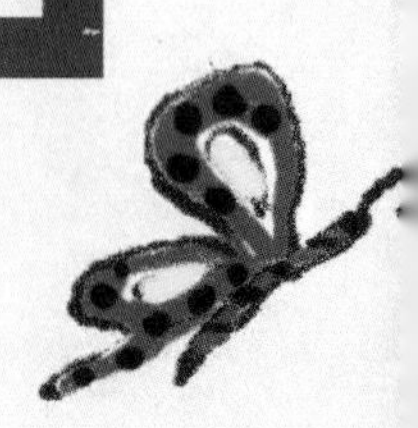

Forever Friends

For Makalya Joy, Muriel, and Jim Sitton

by Sandra Baran

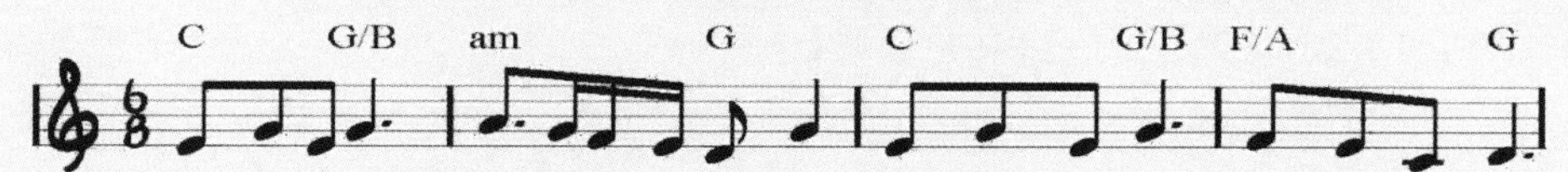

1.For-ev-er friends hap-p'ly ev-er af - ter, For - ev - er friends car - ing we'll be
2.For -ev-er Friend God, is al-ways wat-ching Hol-ding your hand, guid-ing your way.

Bears and un - i - corns cas- tles and laugh- ter For-ev-er friends ev-er we'll be. Your
As you walk a-long, strong and cour a- geous, For-ev-er Friend

with you each day. Un-i-corn cas- tles un-rea-cha-ble dreams, no-thing's im-pos-si- ble

as_ it seems, Al-ways keep rea - ching, keep trus-ting keep hope in your heart_ your

heart. For-ev-er friends hap-p'ly ev-er af- ter For-ev-er friends

car-ing we'll be Bears and un-i- corns cas- tles and laugh- ter For-ev-er friends

ev- er we'll be. And pre-cious in God's eyes al- ways you'll be.

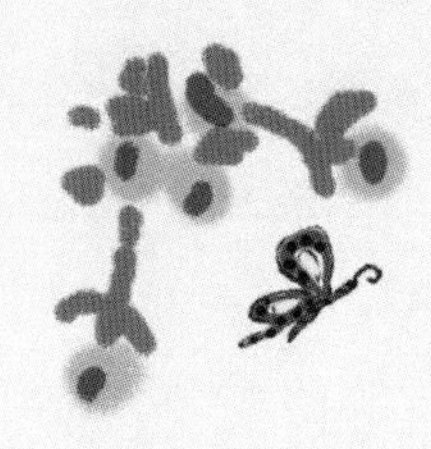

SPECIAL TOUCHES IN THIS BOOK

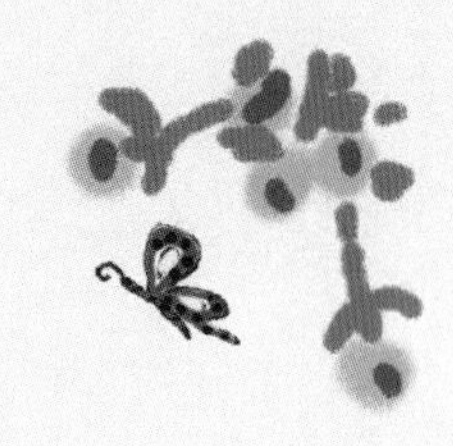

Makayla loved to personalize her books with special "To" and "From" designs. This is her actual drawing from one of her books.

Makayla Joy Sitton

This is Makayla's very own signature. She taught herself italic from a 1777 primer book of Bible verses and poetry. She loved to make her writing beautiful.

Makayla loved to listen to audio books. So we decided to share her actual recording of "The Bear's Castle". Now you can enjoy reading along with her.

My Notes

Makayla loved to journal and write. So we included "MY Notes" pages so you can write and journal too.

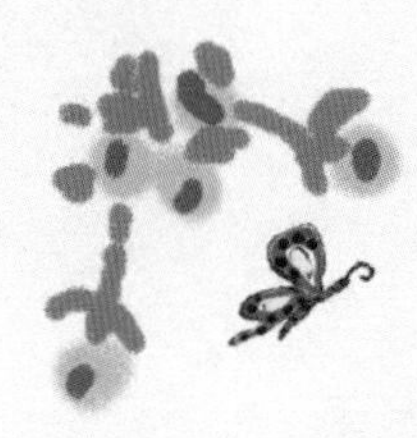

SPECIAL TOUCHES

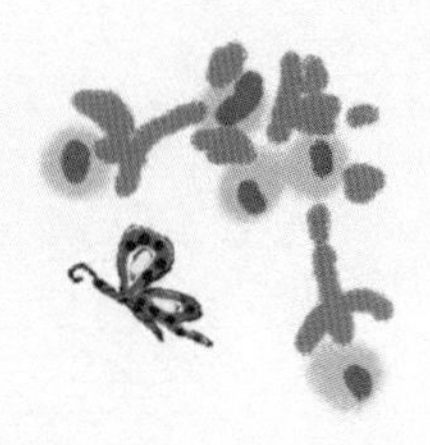

Little Bear's bedroom is very much like Makayla's. Here is an actual picture of Makayla's bedroom. Can you spot the things that are the same?

My Notes

Tyler is a professional illustrator and artist of book covers and children's book illustrations. Tyler illustrated this book for Makayla Joy Sitton and her parents, Jim and Muriel, out of the deep bond of losing a child.

Tyler wrote in memory of her daughter, Heather, who was courageous, beautiful, kindhearted, intelligent, and ran Kats N Kittens Adoption and Rescue. The children's book, "Second Chance- A True Story of Hope", is about how one little cat was abandoned, rescued and found a happy ending and a loving home through a cat shelter and is an invaluable tool for helping a child learn the consequences of casual pet ownership. This story is told by the cat, from his viewpoint, so it has a way of putting you into his world and his experiences.

Profits are donated to pet rescues. Tyler's book is available on Amazon under "Tyler Hollis".

You may visit her website at:
www.childrensbookillustrator-tylerhollis.com

SECOND CHANCE
A True Story Of Hope
Tyler Hollis

SANDRA

Sandra Baran embarked upon the adventure of teaching piano to Makayla when Makayla was just four years old. They had many wondrous and joy-filled times together.

Composing the music for "The Bear's Castle" was an inspirational journey for Sandra. She created the beautiful melody called "Forever Friends". She also produced the fun musical themes for "Little Bear" "the Unicorn", and "the Castle".

Sandra has been a teacher, performer, accompanist and church musician since her teenage years in New Jersey. She began her music studies at the age of five with her father and grandfather. Ms. Baran is now founder and director of the Jupiter Academy of Music. She composes and continues to perform in South Florida both as a pianist and vocalist.

Thanks to the Makayla Joy Sitton Foundation scholarships, students who would not ordinarily be studying music will receive the wonderful gift of music.

Proceeds from this book will go to the Makayla Joy Sitton Foundation which provides funding for music, dance, and literacy scholarships. The Foundation's mission is to help other children enjoy the arts in the same way Makayla did.

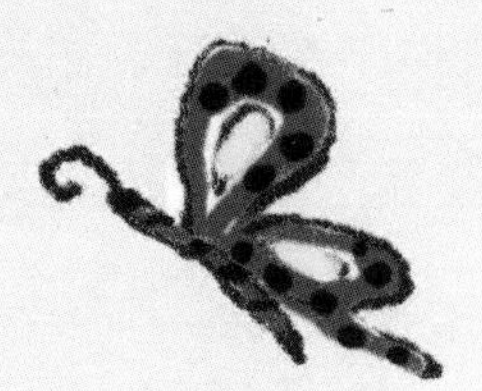

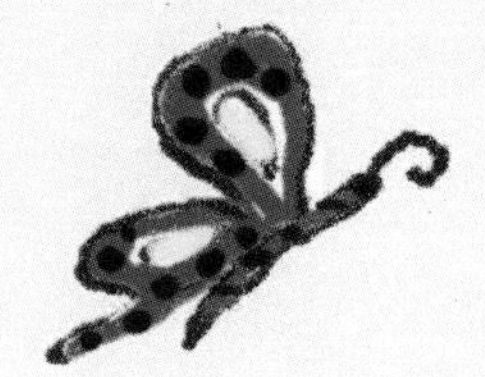

Made in the USA
Lexington, KY
05 January 2011